The Town Where No One has Ever Seen a Murder

Mojaffor Hossain

Translated by Marzia Rahman

This hardcover edition contains thirty flash fiction pieces originally written in Bengali by Mojaffor Hossain and translated into English by Marzia Rahman.

Published by,Doshor Publications, 17/1D, Surya Sen Street, Second Floor, College Square,

Kolkata – 700012, India

Website- www.doshorpublications.com[1]

First hardcover edition published in January 2026

ISBN: 978-81-996527-4-3

1. http://www.doshorpublications.com

Dedication

"To my daughter, Zakira Noor, who makes me proud every day."

Translator's Note

I first encountered Mojaffor Hossain's stories through their unsettling quietness. They are brief, often deceptively simple, like Robert Frost's poems, yet they continue to echo in the reader's mind long after they end. As a flash fiction writer myself, I was immediately drawn to his work and wanted to translate it into English. What began as a modest attempt to translate a handful of stories soon gained new momentum when one of the stories, *Even Though I Am Against Murder, I Have Murdered Someone*, was nominated for a Pushcart Prize by the U.S.-based magazine *Chewers by Masticadores*. That recognition reinforced what I already sensed as a reader: that these stories, though rooted in a specific language and place, had the power to travel.

After I brought together thirty of Mojaffor Hossain's flash fiction pieces into a collection, I discussed possible titles with the author, and together we considered several options. In the end, we chose *The Town Where No One Has Ever Seen a Murder*, a title suggested by the editorial team of Doshor Publications. This title is important because it captures the spirit and underlying tension of the book. At first glance, the title sounds calm, even reassuring. A town where no one has ever seen a murder suggests safety, order, and moral stability. However, as the stories unfold, this sense of certainty begins to crack. The title reflects the central idea of the collection: the gap between what people believe about themselves and their world, and what actually happens beneath the surface. This tension between appearance and reality, belief and action, runs throughout the book.

The stories in this collection come from ordinary worlds, yet they are shaped by strange and unexpected situations in which logic often breaks down and moral certainty disappears. Faith clashes with desire, love turns into violence, and right and wrong are no longer clear. A man who believes in strong principles commits a terrible act. A man without a shadow steals the shadows of others. An unborn child tells the story of his own death. These moments are not meant to shock the reader, but to reveal hidden truths about society and human behavior.

Most of the characters in these stories are ordinary people: teachers, lovers, sons, daughters, villagers. Yet they find themselves in extreme situations that expose injustice and inequality. Themes such as class exploitation, corruption, and moral hypocrisy appear again and again, often told with irony or dark humor.

Love is also shown in difficult and uncomfortable ways. It is often secret, painful, or incomplete. A character named Ira appears in several stories, carrying feelings of loss and longing. Through her and others, the stories explore intimacy and show how love can exist alongside fear, regret, and guilt.

Although these stories are rooted in South Asian society, they are not limited to one place. They move between villages and cities, between old myths and modern life, and between personal experience and political reality. The stories are very short by design. Each one can be read quickly, but it is meant to stay in the reader's mind long after.

Translating *The Town Where No One Has Ever Seen a Murder* was not only a matter of changing words from one language to another. It was also an imaginative task. I tried to remain faithful to the emotional precision and strangeness of the original texts. Hossain's writing is simple and direct. His language is spare, his images are vivid, and his tone is often calm even when the events are disturbing. One of the central challenges of translation was to preserve this balance: to resist explaining too much or making the stories more "accessible" at the cost of their ambiguity. These narratives depend as much on what is left unsaid as on what is stated directly.

The social and cultural background of the stories is specific to South Asia, shaped by issues of class, gender, faith, and power. Still, their emotional meaning is universal. Rather than overburdening the text with explanations or cultural glosses, I trusted the stories to speak for themselves, allowing readers to encounter unfamiliar worlds with the same sense of curiosity that I felt when reading them in the original language.

Another challenge was translating the author's use of surrealism and dark humor. These elements are quiet and subtle. They appear naturally, without warning. In English, I tried to keep this same tone so that the strange moments would feel surprising but not forced.

What stayed with me most during the translation was the author's compassion for his characters. Even when they make cruel or harmful choices, the stories do not judge them harshly. They also do not offer comfort or clear answers. Instead, they invite readers to live with uncertainty and to think about how fragile human lives and moral choices can be.

This translation is my attempt to carry Mojaffor Hossain's voice across languages without changing or softening it. Any mistakes that remain are entirely my own. I hope readers will enjoy these stories as much as I enjoyed translating them, a process that also helped me grow as a writer. I believe English-language readers will find in these stories the same unsettling beauty, sharp irony, and deep humanity that moved me to translate them.

The Distance

The morning fog lingers all day. Or is that my imagination? Once, the sun didn't rise for seven days straight. The municipal lights across the city grew so exhausted that they fell asleep. I have never minded the darkness. But when I told Ira how I spent those seven days in the dark, she insisted nothing like that had ever happened. But it did happen to us. And Ira witnessed it too.

During those seven days, we were in a comma.

In that blurred, half-awake existence, I search for Ira. She always understood truth and lies better than I ever could. But now she lives at the far edge of my solitude, and only in the hollow of loneliness can we meet face to face.

Ira comes. *The light is too bright today*, she says. The line of light stretches farther and farther until the night dissolved into a void. I don't mention the fog again. We see the world differently now. I sit in the mist, Ira in the light; both so intense that we can't see each other clearly.

It's our distance that brings us closer. Does Ira know that? Is this why we deliberately stay away from each other?

She is so far away that I can't even ask her, *Ira, how are you?* A butterfly that once wandered freely through flowers and fields now finds itself stranded in a city without trees, trapped in a room with no window. *Ira, how can I reach you?*

***

Face to Face

"We got married," the man said. "In the winter, five years ago."

"Okay. A lot of weddings take place in winter. I got married in winter too," I said.

"She left me in the summer. It was very hot that day," he said.

"Divorce? There are too many divorces nowadays. It doesn't matter if it's winter or summer. It's the destructive side of women's empowerment, once women start earning, families start breaking. Too many families fall apart these days."

"No, not divorce," the man replied in a slightly grumpy tone.

"Extra marital affair? It happens all the time. Having an affair with a friend or a boss is practically normal these days. In many cases, wives and daughters even sleep or run away with the driver. Too many cases," I said encouragingly.

"Not that either," the man said. "Death." He stared ahead, annoyed, as if death itself were an inconvenience.

"Accident? There are too many deaths on the road. Nearly sixty-four people die in accidents every day. Can you imagine?" I said happily, as though we were not talking about death but something amusing."

"No. Murder," the man replied unmindfully.

"Is that so? Was it looters? It happens a lot in the city, in alleys, *gullies*, even on the main roads. Even in broad daylight. Murders have risen too. One can get killed just for slapping someone. It's a daily occurrence," I said, trying to comfort him.

"I killed her," the man said in a calm voice. "The driver is a proven killer. He is in prison now." He stopped speaking and looked toward a young girl coming out of a shopping mall across the street. I stand still, transfixed. The girl crossed the road and walked straight toward the man.

With a smile on his face, the man said to the girl or perhaps to me, "We'll get married some winter." "Let's watch that movie again," the girl said cheerfully as she held my hand.

The man vanished in an instant. *Watching a movie or simply having fun with a driver's wife is a rare thing in the city. It almost never happens. Why does it happen so rarely?* I wondered as we walked toward the narrow alley leading to the movie theatre.

In Zero Gravity

I sit for hours. Nothing to look forward to, nothing to look back on. At times, I wish I could flee this house altogether, grabbing the courtyard in my palms. But where would I go? There is nothing to look forward to. There is no urge to turn back.

"Ma is crying," Morium says as she comes in. She is my aunt's daughter. Mother brought her here after my aunt was killed by her husband, my uncle. Little Morium delivers the news and slips away again.

I won't go to her; I tell myself I'll go if something else happens. After a while, I rise, then sit down again. I don't like sitting here, but I don't like dragging this body up and walking either. So I stay put, separating my body and mind. Once separated, I watch my mind to see whether it can leave on its own. It can but it doesn't.

It sits beside me instead, leaning against my body. Another version of me is formed between the body and the mind – to see the two together. For the first time I realise I can go on without thinking at all. Thoughts can be held at zero. But without thoughts, time becomes inert. Soon, I feel as though I've been sitting here forever, with nowhere to go.

Morium returns. "Ma is dead," she tells me. I feel nothing. Ma had been threatening suicide for some time, trying to frighten Baba. He never cared. None of us took her threats seriously either. There has never been much difference between Ma and the guava tree in the courtyard. If she killed herself, that would prove a difference at last. But the truth is she actually saved herself by dying. Morium leaves.

Seeing Morium hop like a kid, I forget about Ma. I don't feel anything for anyone, anymore. I remember the day Morium's body was found under a pile of rice straw. There were no marks on her body. It was Ma who noticed her red half-pant first, "How did it turn red?" she shouted. A drunken Baba lay beside the pile. I can't recall if I felt anything that day.

When you feel neither good nor bad about anything, you can sit like this for eternity. Ma comes and sits beside me. Watching me, she separates her body from her mind. From now on, she, too, won't feel good or bad about anything.

***

The Last Letter

I kept only one letter out of many. And yet, it felt as though I had hidden you somewhere in the house. When the man pulled at the pillow, I feared he might find you. If he bent down to look under the bed, I wondered whether you were there. When he opened the wardrobe, I felt he would cry out upon seeing you inside. It felt as if I had hidden you everywhere – inside the drawer, between the pages of a notepad, behind the door.

A single letter, proof of your existence, left me vulnerable, exposed. I stayed awake at night. I was startled every now and then. I couldn't take it anymore. I had to free myself even from your last memento. It was just a one-page letter with a few random words. You had sent a simple message. That you had been posted abroad, and you were leaving. *Stay well,* you wrote at the end. I didn't know why I kept the letter. Maybe I thought it wouldn't hurt me if it ever ended up in his hands. But I couldn't keep it. I tore it into a thousand pieces, so many that no one could ever piece the words together again. Then I lit a match; it burned in my hand.

It was your last letter. I had to tear it up, yet I could neither throw it away nor burn it. I remembered how you once told me that during a school exam, while cheating, you panicked and swallowed the scrap of paper. *Do you remember?*

***

At the Birth of Death

One sits in silence. Her eyes blink occasionally. Sometimes her lips tremble, sometimes they do not. A lizard climbs her shoulder, mistaking her for a statue. Only memories pierce the stillness of her mind and body – memories of losing her father, mother, and brother, and of her house burning. Nothing else remains before or after that moment. Only a few minutes from her fifteen-year-old past linger in her memory, replaying endlessly.

One talks nonstop. Words pour out as they come, sometimes escaping her lips before they even reach her mind. Sometimes she seizes random words midair. Yet she says nothing about herself or about anyone else. Instead, she talks of monsoons, rivers, a pair of kittens, jam-jarul fruits, and a few sour berries. The sun shower, the evening star, children playing with dolls. Each day she brings up a new topic, forgets it, and the next day begins again with another.

One cries; she keeps crying. Awake or asleep, sitting or lying down, the tears never stop. She cries when she speaks, when she eats, when she laughs. It is as if she does not live by breathing, but by crying.

The one who laughs keeps laughing. Sometimes it goes on endlessly; sometimes she pauses to catch her breath. Others don't join her. Her laughter doesn't sprinkle light like diamonds. It spreads all over the room but makes no sound; it hits the cruel wall and returns to her like a rock. And she smiles the same smile back and forth.

There is one who neither laughs nor cries, she cannot sit at ease either. She looks anxious, restless, fidgeting endlessly like a headless chicken. It is as if someone had thrown her into fire or left her in water without teaching her to swim. Or forced her to walk on slippery ice. At times, it seems she is lying on a bed of broken glass or sitting surrounded by snakes and worms.

Their eyes are open. Their eyes are closed. Their legs are spread. There are blood clots on their legs, fresh blood, dried blood. Their legs are lifeless like wood, as heavy as stone. If they use all their strength, they can move only a little as if pushing tons of weight. They have no strength left in their bodies. They wait in the camp – but for what, they don't know. Those who become pregnant are dragged outside and killed outright. Others are killed slowly – through rape, beatings, or starvation.

But what will happen after the war?

No one dares to ask the question. Not even to each other. If the question peeks into someone's mind, others huddle in fear. Life is such that death seems kinder, even inviting.

This is how they live amidst death and die amidst life – legs spread apart.

***

Even Though I am Against Murder, I have Murdered Someone

Shila says, "It's not a big deal to kill someone."

I listen in silence.

"Everyone should have the right to murder once," she adds.

I still say nothing.

Shila continues, "Those who become killers commit many murders. But even those who have never killed feel the urge at some point.

"You know I'm against killing," I reply. "That's why I don't support religious wars."

"Murder is an everyday event. People have been killed in the name of the country, nationalism, religion, or simply the demands of the moment. There are also people who kill for personal reasons in addition to these collective killings. The history of murder is as old as life itself. As we speak, hundreds are being killed right now. The state kills, society kills, committees kill, people kill. A killer takes a life and then may be killed in a crossfire."

There is logic in Shila's words. But I could never kill anyone.

"He who cannot justify the right to kill should question his own right to live." Shila's words strike me, as if spoken directly to me.

"A coward like you can never be a patriot, Shila says. "You won't kill anyone even when the situation demands it. The state, society, and people always teach you to murder. Someone might be killed right beside you, and one day you will die too, without ever killing anyone in your life. Maybe someone will kill you, or maybe you'll die of a heart attack. When people will hear about your death, they will say you died of old age. What could be more frustrating than this?"

I can't stand her anymore. I get riled up. Talking about murder does not suit a well-educated, cultured woman like Shila. It's not only humans, I abhor all kinds of killing. I often speak about the rights of trees to live. But Shila wants me to commit a murder. If she stays any longer, I will kill the man. It would even benefit us. Yet killing is not in my nature. I need to stop Shila. If I let her go on, she might turn me into a killer. No, I cannot become a murderer. I must stop her.

Still. Silent. Shila won't speak again.

I go to the bathroom to wash my hands. *A man can kill once* – if Shila were alive, I could tell her that.

***

Her Cries are Like the Sound of River

"I waited for you that day. I left the first train and took the next one. You didn't come. There was no way I could go back," says Ira.

I look the other way. She will never know the real story. She will only know that I didn't show up. That I didn't keep the last word I'd given to her. I don't know whether she is happy or not in her life; if not, it's on me. And this lack of knowledge made me carry the burden all these years.

This is why, perhaps, I don't ask her anything. After looking for her all these years, after all the prayers, it suddenly feels as if it'd have been better if we haven't met. The search itself makes up for the rewards sometimes.

"I am fine. I am at least breathing. I left my home for you. For love. I had to pretend to be in love many times later in life in order to survive. Yes, it was all acting. You wanted to do the same, but you failed. Your love was pure, but the rest was fake. If I didn't have this faith in you, I wouldn't have survived. One needs faith to live," Ira says.

We sit with our backs against the river. The night turns darker. I wanted to hold Ira's hand and cry. But I can't.

"Your silence says a lot of things," Ira says. "You don't have to say anything else." Ira is more mature now. I don't know what life has given her, but it surely has taught her how to read the language of silence.

I feel relieved; I don't have to say anything. Ira cries. Her cry mixes with the sound of the river.

"My life would have been different if you came that day," Ira says. "Only death could save me, but it didn't come either. I was never destined to live a free life. It was probably my luck that you didn't come. You were not responsible for that, what happened was just a pretext."

It was such a pretext that cost me more than you. You are still alive. In spite of all the struggles and hardships, you are alive. But someone who is not alive can't even experience the pain. I can't tell Ira. *That day, I left for the station. And I'd have reached before Ira if everything went smoothly. But my motorcycle came under the wheels of a truck.*

The tea seller boy comes. He serves one cup of tea. "Won't you give him?" Ira hints at me.

"Whom? I can't see anyone."

Ira doesn't reply. She stares at me with eyes full of tears.

***

Proximity in Distance

"Will you hold my hand?" I heard Baba ask.

My hands began to tremble. I couldn't gather the courage to touch him.

We kept walking. "You don't like it there?" I asked. "Do you?"

"The only advantage is that I can come whenever I want. I couldn't do that before. You live so far away; you couldn't come either. But now, we can take walks in your town. Do I take too much of your time? Time is sold here at the cost of life."

"You never took my time; you gave it to me," I said. "You're here today because I needed you. I can't talk freely to anyone here. My wife and son cannot speak Bangla. I speak their language. I have no one to share my thoughts with, Baba."

"You know, for people like you, staying well is an art. You have to adopt it. Only fools can be happy without any reason."

"It would be better if I were a fool," I said. "Then I wouldn't have come here. A stupid son might not have made you proud, but at least we could have stayed together."

"There's no point thinking about that and feeling sad," Baba replied. "That's why I told you earlier, you need tactics to stay happy."

"I didn't know anything: how you and Ma lived, what you ate, when you slept, what you talked about. You suffered so much in the hospital, didn't you? I tried hard to get leave from the office; you know that. When the news came, I was in a crucial meeting, taking notes from my boss. Even a small mistake could have cost me heavily."

"No one asked for your explanation," Baba said with a sigh.

"It would have been easier if someone else had asked the question. Questioning oneself is far more difficult, it chokes one from the inside. Sometimes I feel as if I'm trapped in a box of light filled with oxygen. As if I am slowly drowning. I'm alive, yet I cannot taste life. In those moments, you usually come; I can sense your presence. I see your voice shimmering before my eyes. I feel alive again, remembering the bygone days."

Baba laughed. I could hear Baba's laughter even among all the sounds. His childlike chuckle seemed to gather on the horizon and spread across the entire sky. I no longer felt like a stranger among the unfamiliar trees, birds, and people.

"It would be wonderful If Ma could come," I said.

"She will come too. One cannot come to such a faraway land on a whim unless one dies. But It won't be long." As Baba said this, he stood still. I sensed he wanted to say something; he tried very hard, but no words came out. It felt as though someone had clogged his mouth forever. Baba stared at me, blankly, silently.

***

Let it Be

I used to think I'd tell her someday: *not all love is the same. You can declare love at any moment in life, even when it promises no home.* But what I didn't realise is that time reveals everything, eventually. I don't know why I ever thought time was mute.

Now, standing before Ira after fifteen years, I find myself unable to say anything at all. I could say it now – every word I rehearsed, every truth I carried. But Ira already seems to know everything. For how long? I almost ask, but some questions prefer to remain questions.

I could unburden myself by telling her, yet I can't. Not after all these years, I can't blurt out the words I saved.

I call her. "Hello," she says.

We didn't have mobile phones back then. So this is the first time I am hearing her voice from a distance. For a moment, I'm not sure it's really Ira. And as soon as the doubt creeps in, I forget what I wanted to say. I tell myself I'll say it the next time I see her. Time, of course, only smiles quietly.

My mother once asked me, "What do you want?" I couldn't tell her. I thought I'd tell her later. Time laughed the same way back then too. I could never tell Ma what I wanted. She died on one such beautiful afternoon which took me a long time to process. Now that she is gone, I can no longer figure out what I truly want. The question remains. Sometimes I feel she probably took the answer with her. I rush to her at that half-asleep dawn. I stand close to the parting of her hair, and I forget the question.

Ma, what do I want? Whenever I am about to ask her, a fear rises in me that knowing that the answer might sever my ties with her. Ma should keep something that belongs to me.

And when time laughs in the same familiar way today, I think to myself: *let it be, Ira.* Some words are meant to remain unsaid, stored carefully so that the memories do not fade.

***

Waiting for the Rain to Stop

"It's raining," I tell Ira. I'm not sure how long we have been standing side by side. We should say something. Time stands still when you don't speak.

Ira and I live in eternal silence now. Once, on a half-finished afternoon, we promised that one of us would always break the silence. One of us never kept that promise. To push that stalled moment forward, I begin the conversation. It starts with a wrong sentence though. It is not raining. There is no sign of clouds in the sky.

Still, Ira says, "Hmm." Then she asks, "Why didn't you tell me?"

After all these years, I can't remember. *Why didn't I tell her?* I ask myself. One single word. I thought I told her.

I stand silently. Will it sound irrelevant if I say it now? I should have told her long ago. Ira has to leave. Another household is waiting for her. Someone is waiting for me too. We could never return home together, never to the same address.

"You could have said it too?" I ask.

Ira stands silently.

Some questions remain unanswered. Because we couldn't tell each other in time, we can't now. The question drifts between us, hovering in our eyes and faces.

Ira will leave now. I should leave too. We don't know the language of parting. We head in two different directions. Behind us, two shadows linger in the place where we stood moments ago, waiting for the rain to stop.

***

There are No Lines Written for Us

I've told you before, "Don't try to become a character in this story. Someone else has written it, and I am only a guest character – sometimes visible, sometimes not." Ira suppresses a laugh. She has a beautiful smile, but she looks even more beautiful when she hides it.

"If we want, we can start our own story. The characters will write their own paths. It can happen. It does happen," Ira says.

"To do that, we'd have to step out of the story we're in now. So many stories in this world are left unfinished. People like us who end up as characters in someone else's narrative are afraid of getting trapped in an incomplete or unwritten story for the rest of our lives." I speak to Ira quietly behind the writer's back.

The writer of this story has placed us in a tea stall. Ira enters with the heroine. The hero and I have been waiting for a while. It will be a three-minute scene: the hero and heroine will speak, and we two will sit in silence. No lines are written for us. Ira and I communicate with our eyes. We will write our own story. We will be the main characters. Ira says she doesn't mind sharing the screen with me in the lead roles.

I had the same conversation with Mithila before. But the writer killed her at the end of the story. Mithila died in a road accident; the heroine of the story survived. The writer didn't have to kill Mithila, but he did. He was the writer, so he could do that.

Later, I lost two more women. Among the two, Silvia is still alive. But she won't be the heroine of my story. The writer got her married and sent her to the USA. Silvia won't return. I could have asked her but why would she return from a story that gave her freedom? Silvia is not stupid.

People like us who become the characters of other people's story value freedom a lot. Those who write or read the story won't realise it.

"If you were not a character, we wouldn't have known each other well," Ira says. "We met at the last scene of a story. We meet again today in another story. It's at the beginning of the story this time," Ira says.

But I feel uncomfortable as a guest character. I won't be there till the end. "Will you be there?" I wanted to know.

Ira says nothing.

"I am happy that you have got the complete role."

Ira still says nothing.

"The woman you're staring at is Ira. She has cancer, only a few days left," the hero whispers into my ear.

I stare at Ira. Speechless.

Ira stares at me. Speechless.

There are no lines written for us.

***

Once there was a River Here

"The river is quiet today. I have never seen it like this before," Baba says.

I don't say anything. We sit in silence for a long time. At one point, Baba raises his hand to hint something in the distance. "See, the boat there. We had a boat like this. We used to go fishing. Back then, there was more water in the river. In the monsoon, the water rose up to this point where we're sitting now. There is less water now. I have never seen this river so quite before. This is not a good sign. A storm is coming." Baba keeps talking. "Look, the fisherman can't catch a fish; the bird will pluck up one for sure. See, it pecks a fish in one fell swoop. Let's go." Baba says. "We will come to see the river some other day. Oh, Let me do *wudu*. Your grandfather used to do *wudu* here."

"Do it some other day. You just said the sign is not good. There might be a storm," I tell father.

"Yes, right. Have you seen how it bellows like a bull? Let's go then."

We get up. Baba raises his hand suddenly and shouts, "Aree, are you stupid? Bring the boat to the bank. A storm is coming."

I take Baba by the hand. A couple of young boys pass by, running towards the river. Baba shouts again, "Don't go to the river. You will drown."

I drag Baba forcefully. Behind us, the boys ran with kites in hand along the slim parting road in the vast barren field.

***

The Existential Crisis of the River

It was a little far from our house. I used to go there every morning or evening, though I don't remember why. One afternoon, I set out as usual, but something strange had happened: the river was gone. Who could have made such a big river disappear overnight? Distraught, I returned and asked my mother, "Ma, can you tell me where the river is? I can't find it anywhere."

Ma laughed and said, "You lost a mountain a few days ago. Now it's a river. I don't know what to do with you."

I remembered the mountain then. I used to climb it a little every day, starting the next day from where I had stopped the day before. One day, I forgot to climb down.

I said to Ma, "I can't come down."

Ma said, "Forget it."

I had to forget the mountain. Later, I couldn't find it again.

My relentless search led me to the river. Someone had sown a seed of forgotten history in its waters which bloomed like a story with the evening light. And when it bloomed, it melted back into the water. I put all my effort into learning how to read that fleeting story.

When I told Ma about it, she said, "The day you find my story floating in the water, I won't be here anymore. When people die, they become a story in the river."

I felt very sad that day. Standing by the river, I watched people turning into stories.

Though I had never seen them before, I knew who they were. They called me by their children's name. I searched for my mother among them. How strange it felt! At one point, I even prayed for her death, just to see her story drift into the river. I never told her this. Even though we spoke about many things while sitting near the *kolpaar*, as the night slowly peeled itself away from the day, I kept this thought to myself.

When I couldn't find the river today, I kept thinking. The river had been here; it was supposed to be here forever. I hadn't created it. Perhaps it wasn't here because I couldn't make anyone else believe it. Many paths vanish like this when you see it alone. I once told Ma, *if only I could make people see everything I've seen.* She laughed at first but then turned sad. "Then you will have less things to see," she said.

I don't feel sad anymore. I know the river exists somewhere. It is not here because no one accepts it. But it exists, just as Ma does. She became a story six months and ten days after I was born; and everyone knows that.

***

Waiting for Death, Not Immortality

We waited for death. We stood there year after year. We had heard that immortality could be attained after dying. But we were not waiting for immortality. It was death itself we longed for.

Why did we want it? None of us can remember anymore. We prayed for death for some unknown reason a long time ago and came to stand here. Perhaps, none of us wished to live any longer. Or maybe we had lost faith in life and decided to die. Was our existence meaningless? Or was it the futile drag of time that pulled us towards this place? Sometimes we wonder if we should go back, search for the reason. But to go back would mean remembering, and remembering would only bring us here again. That thought alone keeps us rooted where we are. The only thing we know for certain is this: we came here because life seemed pointless. And now, we will wait. We will wait year after year. No matter what a man desires, he cannot live forever. Eventually, our waiting will end.

Then, one day, our faith falters. Someone says, "Are we dead? Years ago, did we die in some war or some fight?"

Doubt creeps into our minds. We try to remember any event or accident in which we might have died. We gather our scattered memories together in this infertile land. Perhaps a barren tree can still grow out of barren memory. So we wait, empty-minded, hoping to witness some divine revelation. Memories get free. And we realise that while we remain inert without memories, memories themselves can stay alive without us. If lives differ from one another, perhaps deaths differ too. How can I be certain that my father and mother share the same death?

Maybe this is why we wait – for death, not immortality.

***

The Butterflies Fade Away as Colourless Clouds

The butterflies fade away as colourless clouds, Himel copies this sentence in his notebook from the *jhal muri* packet. Then he sticks it to his table. Hira sits next to him. She looks sad, wondering whether to tell Ma about the incident.

"What have you written today?" Hira asks.

"Read it yourself." Himel replies. "You won't get it. Guaranteed!"

Hira sits on the bed, facing the window. Without changing her position, she turns her head and throws it a glance.

"It's good. It reflects my mind." She said, staring at the void.

"Did you get it, apu? Really?" Himel asks with surprise in his eyes.

"No."

"Then why did you say that it was what you felt?"

"Is it possible to read everything that passes through one's mind?" Hira pauses. After a while, she says, "Forget it, no point in telling you all this. You won't understand."

"Choto Chacha entered your room in the afternoon. I know that. He asked me about you. I told him that you were on the first floor," Himel stops here.

Hira is about to say something but decides against it and sits quietly. Himel doesn't take it further either. The two siblings sit with their backs to each other, one on the chair and the other on the bed. The door and window across the room are open, a windy breeze storms through the house. The air is hot though. Droplets of sweat gather in the waves of Hira's cleavage – they look like fleeting dewdrops on grass blades after a drizzle.

"Choto Chacha wanted to wipe off your sweat," Himel says.

"How did you know?" Hira looks at her chest once and asks.

"I watched it behind the door."

"What else did you see?"

"He licked the sweat from your forehead. I didn't step in since you didn't protest."

"He had a knife in his left hand. He would have plunged it into my stomach had I resisted. He warned me."

"I had a knife too. Only if you stopped him once."

"How can I trust someone who can't even kill a rat?"

"You should trust the one who doesn't kill a harmless rat without reason."

"Will you give me the knife?" Hira asks.

"It was right under your bed. It belonged to Apa, our elder sister," Himel says. Then he takes out the knife from his pocket and puts it on the table.

***

The Man Who Wanted a Story

"You'll get some money," I tell the old man. He lives in a shack next to a tea stall at the crossing.

He eats only when someone feeds him; otherwise, he lies around like a tree without a trunk. No one knows for certain when he arrived or where he came from. The oldest man in the neighborhood remembers seeing him once, lying like a dead fish during a rainy season. The villagers even dug a grave for him. He can't recall anything more. But the problem is he keeps inventing new stories about the old man's arrival every day. One day, he came to me and said, "The old man was first seen on a chilling winter morning. An aged man like him sat there without a shirt. Everyone took it casually at the time. But after a few years, people noticed that while everyone else was aging, he wasn't. In fact, he seemed to be growing younger." He had nothing more to say after that.

When I mention the money, the old man tries to recognise me in the fading light. "I haven't worked anywhere for a long time now," he says.

"It was actually me who did the work," I reply. "I wrote your story. You should get a share of the payment I received."

"Which story?" he asks, not reaching for the money.

"I've been watching you from a distance for a while. I wrote a story based on that."

He stays silent for a moment, then asks, "Will you read it to me?"

"It was written without really knowing you. Why would you want to hear it? You might not even like it. It's true that I wouldn't have written it if I hadn't seen you," I try to explain. There is no point in telling a lonely man's story to the lonely man himself. I want to avoid it.

"I don't need money," he says. "Give me a story instead."

"What will you do with a story? And when it's concocted by someone else."

"I can't remember anything," he says. "If I give me a story, I'll make it mine." His eyes glimmer in the dim darkness.

***

I Was Killed Before I Was Born

I was not born yet. I was going to be born in a farmer's family. But I was killed in the womb. No, not by my parents. Those two fools would have died for me a thousand times. Baba had no enemies, no one who would take revenge by killing an unborn child. And who would ever be my mother's enemy! People in ten villages know she has a few loose screws. Still, I became a murder victim. All because of an expired vaccine dose. The government health workers came to our house and injected it into my mother.

Those two fools went to the police station. The officer glared at them and barked, "Do you even know what *date-expired* mean? Who taught you that? The opposition party? Do you have any idea what state power is? Everything is fine. Get out."

Truly, who goes to the government to complain about the government? My parents cowered in fear. Meanwhile, the authorities wanted to be absolutely certain. Baba is in prison now. Ma trembles all the time, muttering, *what if they arrest me?* The poor, crazy woman doesn't understand. I have no limbs. I am not born yet.

If I scream, will the state brand me a traitor? If I leak the news, will they implicate me in a false case – those who signed a dark agreement in broad daylight? If I curse the political leader, will the government take me to remand? I keep searching for my limbs.

The crazy woman burst into laughter. The crazy woman cuts off my invisible limbs.

***

In the Shadow of the Unseen

"I often feel the character that I play has not been written for me. That I have been cast in the wrong part. That is why, perhaps, my own life seems strange to me. I wait for someone to pick this weight off me," Himadri says, throwing away his unlit cigarette.

Nila sits quietly. She starts crying. He has no idea why she is crying. Himadri stares at her.

"Whatever we see comes to us in the shadow of the unseen. We live our entire lives mistaking the shadow for the original, don't we, Himandri?" Nila asks.

Himadri doesn't reply; he takes out another cigarette. He holds the cigarette for some time before throwing it away too. Nile stands up. She has asked Himadri to kill her one night in her sleep. And Himadri has agreed.

It was last night. Police would arrive at their house any time. Himadri had himself dialed 999. He had long wanted to check out this government service. He wanted to know whether it works or not.

After a few attempts, he got through. "Hello, this is Himadri. My address is at 3/3, Ondhogoli, there is a dead body in my house. Please come and settle the matter. And also arrest me." Himadri spoke listlessly.

"Nonsense! Don't make jokes this early in the morning. Someone called a while back asking us to resolve his fight with his wife. Don't we have any other work? What do you think of us?"

"We didn't have a fight. And Nila was not my wife. It's 3/3, Ondhogoli," Himadri said and put down the phone.

"Won't you run away?" Nila asks.

"Where?"

"Wherever you can go. You will go to prison. You might be hanged."

"Let it be. I have no sympathy for a life that is not mine."

***

The Shadow Hijacker

I sit at the station for hours, watching the trains come and go. There is a ticket in my pocket, soaked in sweat. No one is coming here. I am not going anywhere. There is no one in this town left for me to go to. The letter I wrote earlier, with no intention of sending, I tossed into an abandoned pond. And at mid-noon, I slipped away after kissing the young prostitute on the waves of her chest. Beyond that, I'm not leaving anything behind in this town.

I give myself another look, tracing every bend of my body, but my hand melts into nothingness. I look around; I am someone's shadow, waiting alone. No one sees my shadowy existence. I try matching myself to every human body in the station. That is when I realise my own body has left me, searching of another shadow.

Invisible, I wander, looking for a body to make me visible again. Six feet tall, slim and slender, it may vary a little, though no one ever measures a shadow. I need a body urgently. Without one, the girl can't feel my love.

I get off the train and start walking along the footpath. The sun faces me directly. When I look back at the empty road, I realise my shadow is not with me. What a disaster! I rush to the station and search frantically through the crowds. Not a single shadow matches me, neither in shape nor nature.

I take the train back to the town. I will search for the shadow in the alleys and gullies of that town. I compare myself with every shadow along the way. I should have known better, I realise at this point.

At last, when I can't find one that fits, I snatch a shadow from the crowd and flee. I keep a close eye on this shadow. Standing under the sun, I check it again and again. Sometimes I even talk to it. I spend my days adopting to someone else's shadow.

The man whose shadow I stole must have already taken someone else's. And that someone will soon steal from another or maybe even from you ...

***

I will Always Stick to Lies

Ala has done something terribly wrong. He hadn't meant to, something came into his mind suddenly, and before he could stop himself, the truth blurted out. Now the entire family is weeping, as if the house itself has gone into mourning.

"Baba, how could someone make such a huge mistake? How will we face society now?" the elder daughter cries, clinging to her father.

"How can an educated man, a teacher like you, do something like this? We've lost our face, Baba," says the middle son before storming out of the house.

"What will happen to us now?" the youngest daughter cries her heart out, sitting in her mother's lap.

Ala cannot find the words to calm his children. It is true that he has lied all his life, even taught his students to do the same. How, then, come he commit such a grave sin in his old age? His reputation is ruined. One of his three daughters is still unmarried; how will he marry her off? No groom's family would accept a girl whose father has told the truth. What will he do now? And what if, his daughter also starts telling the truth. Ala's mind wanders thinking of this and that.

The Police could arrive at any moment now. Someone has already filed a report at the station. The incident has gone viral on Facebook. A single truth can trigger many things. Ala has spoken the truth in a society that thrives on lies. He has disrupted its discipline. Ala himself once won a district-level medal for his lies. Whom will people believe now?

Whispers swirl through the neighborhood. Ala could have fled the area, but instead he sits in the courtyard. He has come up with a ploy: yes, he told the truth and people heard it, but what if he now denies everything. He will claim they misheard him. It's all a conspiracy against him. He never spoke the truth. He is not some unsocial creature. He has lied his entire life, even won medals for it. He can show the medals to the police if necessary. Everything is part of a plot. People are jealous of him, jealous of his prosperity. That's why they've turned against him. But there is one problem: Alo has already revealed the truth. How is he supposed to hide it now?

***

When All Writers are Immortal

We are gathered to commemorate the death anniversary of a renowned Bengali author. The main speaker, a well-known writer himself, presents an essay, and we listen with apt attention. He explains why the author remains relevant even a century after his death. His novels depict the contempt and disregard that a patriarchal society has shown toward women. A situation that persists even today. In addition, his prose and novels portray sectarianism with remarkable clarity. As we read his work, it often feels as if we are listening to the voice of a contemporary writer protesting against injustice. His depictions of a superstitious society are so vivid that a modern reader might mistake them for commentary on today's world. For these reasons, the speaker argues, the author should be celebrated not only as a modern literary figure but also as a progressive thinker. With this, the speaker concludes his essay.

We begin to clap. The other speakers also support the essayist. The author we are honoring today was a modern writer in his time who remains relevant even hundred years after his death and will remain so for another hundred. He is an immortal writer, they conclude.

When the programme ends, I find my friend standing next to me, laughing. He is not part of the literary world. He came to meet me. Actually, I had invited him for the free food. I feel a twinge of annoyance as I see him making fun of such a serious programme.

"You don't understand literature; I get that. But at least pretend to appreciate it."

"I'm laughing for another reason," he says. "I was thinking about how you and all the big writers here have missed one simple truth."

I feel very angry now. "What is that you understand that none of us did? Let's hear it!"

"What makes this author so far ahead of his time? When Idiots like us are still stuck here. Every writer seems immortal because society lags a century behind. Aren't you ashamed to proclaim that this author will remain relevant a hundred years from now? And while society remains a century behind, what have you writers done in the meantime?"

***

The Big Illness

It's hard to tell from the outside whether it's a hospital or a five-star hotel. Behind it, across the lake, lies a slum with a few houses. It used to be much larger once. No one remembers now whether the construction of the hospital and the shrinking of the slum are connected.

The boy has been coming to the lakeside for the past few days. To pick up bottles with his mother.

"Ma, who lives in that house?" he asks.

"Patients," she replies.

"How does someone become a patient?"

"When people get sick, they become patients and get admitted there?" his mother says, coughing. She has been running a fever for days, her asthma worsening. Despite her poor health, she has to go out to work; she is the sole breadwinner. Since the garment factory shut down, she has been collecting bottles and selling them.

"You often get sick and cry in pain at night. I get stomach aches too. How come we never go there?" the boy asks.

"Not for small sicknesses. People go there when they have a big illness." His mother tries to explain. The boy nods. He understands.

After that, he keeps asking her, "Ma, when will we have a big illness?"

Her asthma worsens that day. She moans through the night and then grows quiet. She lies still, lifeless. One by one, all the sounds retreat from the small room.

Lockdown outside. Police whistles.

From a distance, the neighbours call to him, telling him that his mother is gone.

The naïve boy doesn't understand. "No," he says, "my mother is here. You can't see her from that far."

He cannot understand why no one is allowed to come closer. The army announces instructions through a microphone: "Stay back. Give company from a distance." Their rifles hang heavily from their shoulders.

Seeing them, the boy hides the truth that he hasn't understood anything at all.

People keep trying to make him understand. "*No more* means *dead*," they say.

The boy thinks. He stays quiet for a while. Then his face brightens. "Does my mother have a *big illness* now?" he asks

Those standing at a distance take a few steps farther back.

Climbing onto his mother's still body, the boy looks out the window toward the lake and calls, "Ma, tell me, do you have a big illness now?"

***

The Town Where No One has Ever Seen a Murder

When the murder happened, I was there. I saw it. The faces of the killers are still flashing before my eyes.

What's the name?

I don't know the names, sir, but I know them by face.

Your name?

Hafez Bin Noor.

You've got a beard, I see.

Yes, sir, It's the will of Allah. And my father's teaching.

Yes, it matches. Where have you studied?

Very close, sir, in Hazi Shariatullah... Sir, when the killing...

Isn't it a madrasa? That's what I doubted.

No, sir, government school and college are together. Finishing college, I couldn't study further. Sir, what I was saying, when the killing...

What does it mean you didn't continue your studies?

I was good at Bangla but had all fear for English—Mathematics too.

And in Arabic?

Sir, Arabic, I can read. I've learnt it from my father at home.

That means father and son together?

MashaAllah—as Allah has willed—Abba knows Arabic well and he learnt from my grandfather. Sir, the light fell straight on the murderer's face...

Where did you hatch the plan of killing, then?

Sir, I haven't seen that, but I have seen the murder.

Who else was with you?

Sir, it was only I who have seen this. If anyone were with me, we'd have tried to save the victim.

Was the bomb made at home?

Bomb? No, sir, they killed him with a knife. I myself have seen this.

Was the plan yours or your father made it?

I was returning from the market, sir, but Abba didn't know anything about this. As soon as I stepped in the alley from the main road...

That means you and your father made the bomb attack.

Sir, I'm talking about the murder of Baren Master that occurred in this alley last night.

I'm talking about the bomb attack on the temple last month.

No, sir, we didn't launch any bomb attack. Abba has been blind for a long time. And why on earth should I launch a bomb attack? No, never can I do that, sir.

What were you saying, then?

No, sir, I haven't launched any bomb attack, and neither has Abba. We're innocent.

Not bomb attack, it's a killing that you were talking about.

No, sir, I haven't killed anyone in my life. Astagfirullah, seeking forgiveness from Allah! Why should I kill someone?

Then what about the murder of Baren Master? A Hindu...bearded! Two twos are four, two fours are eight—do you know this multiplication table?

No, sir, I don't know anyone named Baren Master.

Tell the multiplication table of the figure two.

Sir, I didn't see any murder. I wasn't even in the city last night. Trust me, sir.

That's what I believed from the beginning—neither you nor your father saw the murder.

No, sir, Abba is blind. I have the doctor's documents; I can prove it.

Good, very good. Take a cup of tea and then go home straightaway. Blind people don't need to see many things. If the father is blind, the son is blind too, understand? It's science, genetics, not I, that confirms this.

Yes, sir. I'm sorry for the mistake.

***

After the Original Sin

Banga backs out; he won't listen to anyone. He is unflinchingly adamant; he won't allow anyone to touch his young wife, as tender as the shoot of a gourd. He can't bear seeing villagers cut her soft body as tender as the early morning light into pieces and eat them.

Sadly, it has been the ritual for thousands of years. They eat up the burnt flesh of dead bodies and hang some on the *Manda* tree as offerings to Gods and Goddesses. Nothing unusual about it. And Banga has no reason to oppose it. Banga himself had eaten a piece of burnt flesh of Raghu Bagha's mother just two days ago. The *buri* lived to a ripe old age, and her meat was not easy to manage, yet Banga gulped a small piece to avoid antagonizing the Gods who would take it on the old woman. This is how, the sins of the dead body spread in the bodies of those who eat the flesh. This is how the Raghus have been sharing sins of dead people in their clan since ancient times. It's part of their ritual. They believe their sins don't multiply, rather subside if they share someone's sins. And the one who passes away leaves the world as innocent as a lamb to enter the heaven. To them only humans are the most cursed, and the most degenerate creatures on earth. So, the people of the Raghu clan want to be reborn as trees or birds.

Banga stands against the age-old ritual for the first time in their thousand years history. A dissatisfied clan-chief calls for Banga urgently. Putting his wife's dead body inside his house, Banga appears in the court. The Chief tries his utmost to convince him, "Listen, Banga, soil is very sacred; soil is our mother that gives us food and shelter. When the original father and mother of human beings, Adam and Eve, had committed sins and were thrown into the earth, the soil indeed gave shelter and cherished them with warmth and care. Since ancient times, human bodies are prone to sins. Can the innocent and soft soil hold these sins? Now if you bury your wife's dead body, we can't live on well without disasters anymore as we have done for thousands of years. Sins are indeed infectious like devils, and the sins infect soil, eventually causing floods, earthquakes, and destruction of woods . . . Many clans and tribes of the earlier times had been destroyed for this as our forefathers revealed."

Still Banga is firm in his decision. He won't let his beloved wife be gobbled up. He believes his wife is the most beautiful woman the Raghu clan has ever seen. Or they will ever see in the future. He knows that from youths to old men, even the women offered prayers to have his wife intimately. Banga won't let people appease their carnal gratification slurping up the flesh of this coveted woman, no matter she's dead.

At the dead of night, in the darkness, Banga digs a big hole in his room and buries the dead body without informing anyone. In the history of Raghu race, a dead body is buried for the first time.

And for the first time in the history of Raghu race, a massive earthquake shakes the earth.

***

The Hardest War Comes After the Actual War

Hasu has returned. It becomes harder for them to bear, for they mourn his return even more than they mourned his death – a realization that soon dawns on Hasu's mother and wife.

Hasu's brother has been sitting by the dried river since morning. He was the one who raised Hasu after their father's death. At first, seeing Hasu filled him with joy. Then, as if struck by lightning, he startled, before crumpling under the weight of shock. Now, consumed by an endless sense of guilt, he stares at the dried river with tearful eyes.

Mother hasn't said a word. She brushes her hand gently over Hasu's head and slips into the kitchen. She has been sitting there, numb, for a long time. "Go. Take a bath. Do you want something to eat?" she asks after a while. She hands him *lungi* and a *gamcha* and then returns to the kitchen. She can't look him in the eyes.

There are two more houses beside theirs, and a pond. Hasu walks ahead, counting his steps. Seeing him outside, some people stand still, while a few seem to want to speak but cannot find the words. In the end, they simply stare blankly at him. Hasu cowers in guilt for returning alive from the war after so long.

Except one or two young children, no one comes to bathe in the pond so early in the morning. An unknown bride washes clothes with her head covered. Hashu sits with his legs in the water. One or two tilapia lift their heads above the water before diving down again. Something nips Hashu's feet. Life has brought him here: facing a war with no opponent, no injury that can bring death, yet he must keep fighting just to stay alive. Hasu gazes mournfully at a fish, praying for its life with all his heart. Once a front-line fighter, he had been the terror of the enemy, successfully leading numerous operations. And now, that same man sits inertly, ready to surrender. He won't go back home. Where, then, will he go? For the first time, he wonders if it would have been better if the war had never ended.

"Ma, it's been so long since I've seen your face. I want to see you one more time before I leave. I haven't eaten anything cooked by you for so long... I'll have just a bite and go." Sitting alone, Hasu speaks softly to the water in the pond.

You should have written a letter, letting us know you were alive. None of us will know peace now. Don't go, my dear... come back to my heart." Mother speaks to the dying fire in the oven.

"I couldn't go to the war. I ran from village to village to keep our family safe. I couldn't save others while trying to save my own," the elder brother says silently. "Why didn't you come earlier, when you were still alive? What kind of life will you have now?"

The wife is nowhere to be seen. Hasu cannot gather the courage to look for her, afraid his eyes might meet hers. The newborn baby begins to cry. The father of the child is neither Hasu nor the elder brother. It is a war child.

***

Amor Didn't Go to War to Become the Subject of Art

"I went to war, leaving my pregnant wife and mother at home, while you went into a shelter. You weren't there when we needed you the most. And when the war was ended, you began to write anti-war poems. It's your poems that remind people of the war now. No one knows me. You've become immortal while still alive, and I, whether I live or die, don't matter at all. Even though my name is *Amor,* meaning immortal," Amor says.

He is my childhood friend; we now live in different towns.

"Everyone has failures in life. My failure is that I couldn't act as you did when it was required," I say. "But by writing your history, I can fulfill at least some of my responsibilities. Whether it brings me a name or makes the history immortal, well, that remains to be seen."

"A river keeps a locality alive, but the death of a river never becomes history. A locality's history doesn't become the river's history," Amor says this, staring blankly into the distance.

I understand his pain. He lost everything in the war and gained nothing. While I was receiving the national award for my poem *Amor with a Gun in his Hand in a Moonlit Night,* Amor's ancestral land was usurped. The usurper a powerful local chairman took it. The real-life Amor never become famous like the fictional one I had created. Later, I wrote another poem, *Amor is a Minority Now,* fifty years after independence. It, too, was widely appreciated. Whenever minorities come under attack, protesting youth share it on Facebook. Amor watches everything. My creation, Amor, became famous. My friend Amor barely gets a hundred followers. Thousands follow me. I can feel his pain.

"If people utter my name once, they utter yours twenty times because your name appears in every paragraph of my poem," I say hesitantly like a guilty person.

Amor listens without a word. He stays quiet for a long time, then says, "If one day I get evicted from this country, or falsely implicated in some scandal, people will post the same poem on Facebook, won't they? You'll be able to write another poem then. New poem, new fame," he says, his voice listless.

"Don't say things like that, Amor. I feel guilty. My work is to turn events into history, to immortalize a deprived, forgotten freedom fighter like you."

"But I didn't go to war to become the subject of your poem, my friend. I want to live with the rights of a human being. You can be a poet, but you will never realise the pain of being a guinea pig of history; the sorrow of becoming a living fossil. You are the majority. The famous Amor in your poem mocks my existence," Amor says, standing up.

"What about my protest? Does that mean it's untrue too? Couldn't I write poems like everyone else, about birds or the tender smile of a beloved? Even those poems make poets famous nowadays." I try to reason with Amor.

Amor laughs softly. Before leaving, he says, "You won't understand because you are not a minority, my friend, no matter how great an artist you are."

***

The Notes Rustle like Dry Leaves

We took one thousand packets of relief. Some locals agreed to help us. It was decided that one thousand families would be assisted, and we would go and distribute the aid. The journey by truck from Dhaka to Kurigram was exhausting. Moreover, upon reaching there, we found one thousand five hundred people standing in line. We lost our cool. We were told they had been waiting since yesterday. Men and women of all ages, and a few children.

Since there was no way to turn back, we decided to start with the first person in line. We tore open packets and handed out rice or flour to some, sugar to others, and potatoes or flattened rice to a few more. Even then, we couldn't provide for everyone. We gave a little money to some, whatever we had on hand. We feared the deprived might cause a scene, but they left as quietly as they had stood. Watching them walk away empty-handed was unbearably hard.

As we were about to leave this small strip of land rising from the water in our boat, we noticed an old woman waving at us. Her clothes were tattered, and her frail body seemed like it could crumble like a rootless tree in a strong wind. We tried to ignore her. We had nothing left to give. If truth be told, we felt more irritation than pity. We had already distributed everything; why was she calling out to us?

I gathered my courage and stepped a little closer. I needed it; she might be crazy. Standing at a safe distance, I took a hundred taka note from my pocket and gestured toward her. The old woman swayed like a tree but didn't move an inch. She kept waving at me. "I have nothing more. Take it." I shouted. With a sad smile, she waved again. I pulled out another fifty taka note and held it toward her. Still, she didn't move. I felt extremely irritated. I was ready to give her the little money I'd saved for food on my way home, but she wouldn't take it. I lost my temper. I strode up to her and offered her the money. Strange. She didn't take it. My notes stayed in my palm. Then, gathering all her strength, she raised her hands and brushed them over my head and face. I stood silent. I had no words to say. The notes rustled in my hand like dry leaves.

***

Dawn Appears in the Darkness

When the super shop closes, Dipu sits in front of the gate. He sits as still as the plastic plant next to him. He wants to leave, once he tries to leave. Once he stands up. Where will he go? He wonders, then sits down again. Pairing one house with another, passing from one town to the next, hopping across cities, rivers and fields, his mind wanders back to his childhood. The rest of his memories scatter like pieces of a multi-project. Where will he go now? To a house? Whose house? Which house?

Dipu sits for hours on end. The shop opens at 9 a.m. and closes at 8.30 p.m. He preferred it when it used to close at 11. Now he has too much free time. He doesn't need free time. If he could sell his time, he could unburden himself. He thinks of finding another job at night. He could work as a night guard. It's not for the money, quite the opposite. He is willing to pay just to have another job. He takes out his mobile phone from his pocket. He presses the buttons for a while. He holds it to his ear and keeps it there.

"I will send the money, Mother. I'll send it through bKash. Buy all the medicines you need. Don't behave like Abba. No one gets rich by saving money meant for medicine; they just die. Abba died. You stay alive, Ma. What? You need money for Nipa's school fees? Okay, I'll send that too. Ma, do you still have my goat? Did you give away my ball? Ma, I want to come home. One morning, you'll wake up and find me standing near your forehead. I want to come, but I can't remember the way home. Wasn't there a coconut tree near the *kolpar*, the washing area beside the tubewell? Now you'll find a coconut tree in every yard, but no one keeps a *kolpar*. Mother, have you hidden it somewhere? Or did Father take it with him? Ma... Ma..." No reply comes from the other side. Dipu lowers the phone. It hasn't been charged for two days. He put it on the charger earlier but forgot to switch it on. He keeps pressing the button. He feels this, too, is a kind of work.

The buttons seem to be running on a board no different from a mobile keyboard. From 0 to 9, he cannot go beyond them. Within these numbers, he must make his life infinite. He tries to anchor himself there, compressing time in an iota, with no time before or after. And he sits for hours on end.

Dipu stands up. He gathers all his strength, but his legs suddenly become numb. His memories freeze quickly these days. He can't remember anything from even the day before.

When the people in this town think of the future, Dipu constructs his past out of the vacuum of his thoughts. He can't even remember whether he ever had a house. He must have had a mother. If he was born, there must have been a mother. And if there was a mother, there should have been a father too. What about a wife or siblings? He might have them, or he might not. Whenever he thinks of a wife, a child's face flickers out of the blackhole of his memory. If there is a child, there must be a wife too. Or is it his own childhood face? Or someone else's child glowing faintly from the darkness. Are all his loved ones dead? Is he himself alive? Do the dead carry memories?

Dipu imagines himself and everyone else as dead. There is no logic to it. Dipu tries to hear sounds coming from far away. A young bride is crying softly; her pillow is damp with tears. Dipu's senses suddenly sharpen. Everything becomes clear. He rises in bed like an ethereal figure. On the wall above the dressing table hangs a picture frame woven from bamboo. Dipu opens his eyes. Somewhere in this world, he realises, there is a house where his photograph hangs on a wall. But where would he look for such a house?

A dog sits a few steps above him, close to his feet. An empty truck whizzes by. A night bird flies from darkness to darkness. A dream drifts through the town, searching for someone asleep. Here, like Dipu, people either stay awake or plunge into a sleep so heavy that dreams can't reach them. The dreams return empty-handed, carrying only dead souls. One such dead dream now rests in Dipu's hands. He clutches it tightly. But this dream may soon abandon him, proclaiming him dead. And then it will wander off again, looking for another body.

***

Mental

The man gasped and grabbed my hand from behind. I should have been startled, but I was so lost in my thoughts that it took a moment to understand what was happening. He still clutched my wrist. He was panting so hard he couldn't speak. An incident like this should have made me anxious, even afraid. These days, crimes come in endless varieties; every time, the criminals invent new techniques. Only the night before, my son, who studies filmmaking, had sat at the dining table lamenting the loss of his laptop and phone. "Hijackers are more creative than writers and producers now," he had said. "All the wrong people have gone into the wrong professions."

After giving the man a proper look, I felt relieved. He was around fifty, dressed in simple home clothes. He seemed an educated gentleman. Clearly, he was in some kind of trouble. I slipped my hand free from his grip, then held his hand myself. "Calm down," I told him. "Take a few long breaths. I'm in a hurry, but I won't leave until I've heard what you've to say."

But I truly was in a hurry. As the man tried to speak, he kept opening his mouth wide, gulping air. It seemed as though he might swallow all the oxygen around us.

"My wife ..." he began, but couldn't finish.

"What happened to your wife?"

"Crazy."

"Who?"

"My wife. She has mental problems."

"Acha! Please be calm. She'll be fine. Is she seeing a doctor?"

"She won't recover. Come with me," he said, tugging at my hand again.

"I'm not a doctor. How can I help by going there?" I stood firm this time.

"No, you have to come. Otherwise she won't survive." He was one the verge of tears.

"What a mess! But you don't know me, nor does your wife. Why should I go?"

"You'll save her. She is committing suicide." The man began to cry. His legs trembled, and if I hadn't grabbed him in time, he would have collapsed.

"If she is trying to kill herself, shouldn't you be stopping her instead of pulling me around? What a strange man you are!"

"I can't break the door alone. You have to come with me. You'll save my wife. She has mental problems."

At that point, I realised we were wasting precious time by talking. I took him by the arm and began walking in the direction he pointed.

"Why does she want to kill herself?" I asked.

"No reason. She has mental problems. She often attempts suicide," he replied.

"But you can't save her every time."

"Yes. I'm in deep trouble. She understands nothing. She has mental problems."

We began climbing the stairs. It was a four-storey house. I kept thinking I should call for help if we met anyone at the gate or on the stairs; what if the door was too strong to break? But there was no one.

The distance wasn't long, yet the time we spent was enough for someone to attempt dying not once, but ten times.

The door opened the moment I pushed it. I had shoved it harder than necessary. A woman was standing on the other side. She was startled. She took a moment to collect herself and then said, "Again. This happened three times just today. Someday the people on the road will kill us for all the trouble you cause them." As she spoke, she took the man firmly by the arm and made him sit on a chair. The man rested his head on his arm and began fiddling with a glass lid like a little boy. It felt as though the conversation we'd had moments earlier had never happened at all.

A young boy came in and fastened shackles around the man's ankles. I was about to take my leave when the woman said, "This is my elder brother. He has never been married."

***

Haram Halal

As soon as the call to prayer ends, Tuku – Bongo's eight-year-old son stands at the gate of the mosque – every day, at every prayer time. Sheikh Rahim Hafez arrives before the jamaat begins. He hands his expensive wristwatch, mobile phone, and money to Tuku, and then stands in prayer. Tuku waits outside the mosque. After the prayer, Hafez collects his things from Tuku, gives him a five-taka note, and then heads towards Mobu's mango garden. His business is on the other side. From behind this plantation, all the phensedyl arriving from the border is distributed to the nearby towns.

Outside the mango garden, Sheikh Rahim Hafez moves about under a different identity. He is the president of the mosque committee and, more recently, the president of the school committee. What if he himself is illiterate? He is still a respectable person in the village. Ten months ago, he arranged the hiring of a teacher for the school by concealing two lakhs. He always wanted to be the first person in the village to perform Hajj, and he did. But not with illegal money; with halal income, earned rightfully by selling a piece of inherited land. After returning from the Hajj, the first thing he did was hire the teacher. Later, he bought back the land he had sold, this time in his second wife's name. This wife had been nagging him about the land.

After returning from Hajj, he did not miss a prayer. His namaz wouldn't be accepted if he kept the illegal money in his pocket while praying; this is why he hired Tuku, after asking Tuku's baba. For Tuku, this is a job, and the income is not bad for his age. He lives in the Madrasa adjacent to the mosque. After Rahim Hafez leaves, Tuku never forgets to perform his prayer along with those who missed it, or sometimes he prays alone.

When Rahim Hafez was leaving today, handing a five-coin bill to him, Tuku thought for a moment and asked, "Dada, if I take the money from you and then enter the mosque, will my prayer be accepted?

"Why wouldn't it be? With whose money was the mosque built?" Sheikh Rahim Hafez replied, laughing, and then headed towards the mango garden.

**

9 788199 652743

Printed at Repro India Ltd.